Uncle Farley's False Teeth

Uncle Farley's False Teeth

by Alice Walsh
illustrated by Michael Martchenko

Annick Press Ltd.
Toronto • New York

We acknowledge the support of the Canada Council
for the Arts for our publishing program.
We also thank the Ontario Arts Council.

The author thanks Norene Smiley, Sharon Gibson-Palermo,
and Barbara Little for their encouragement and valuable suggestions.

Cataloguing in Publication Data

Walsh, Alice
    Uncle Farley's false teeth

ISBN 1-55037-543-1 (bound) ISBN 1-55037-542-3 (pbk.)

I. Martchenko, Michael. II. Title.

PS8595.A5847U52 1998   jC813'.54   C98-930313-6
PZ7.W34Un 1998

The art in this book was rendered in watercolours.
The text was typeset in Dom Diagonal and Times.

Distributed in Canada by:
Firefly Books Ltd.
3680 Victoria Park Avenue
Willowdale, ON
M2H 3K1

Published in the U.S.A. by Annick Press (U.S.) Ltd.
Distributed in the U.S.A. by:
Firefly Books (U.S.) Inc.
P.O. Box 1338
Ellicott Station
Buffalo, NY 14205

Printed and bound in Canada
by Friesens, Altona, Manitoba.

For Christine

D'Arcy loved Uncle Farley's teeth. Every after-noon, for his three-hour nap, he would flip them right out of his mouth and put them in a glass of water.

One day when D'Arcy heard him snoring, she sneaked into his room, snatched the teeth and ran.

D'Arcy went down to the wharf where her friends were playing. She showed them Uncle Farley's teeth.

"Wow!" said Emma.

"Awesome!" said Kevin.

"Cool!" said Natasha.

"Holy cow!" cried Willie.

But while they were admiring them, the teeth slipped from D'Arcy's hands and fell down into the water. D'Arcy looked, but all she could see was a big fish. It was a fabulous fish, D'Arcy thought. He had a great big tail, and on his fin were little white freckles. But then the fish opened his big mouth, and she saw he was wearing Uncle Farley's teeth.

"Oh, no," said D'Arcy, "I have to get them back!" But the fish swam far out into the ocean.

"I'll get my dad," said Kevin. "He's a fisherman. He'll catch that big fish and get Uncle Farley's teeth back."

Kevin's dad tied a piece of purple bubble gum on a string for bait. "Fish!" he called. And:

The Fabulous Fish with the freckled fin
Swam back into the harbour again
He wore Uncle Farley's teeth as if
They belonged to him.

Kevin tugged, but when he pulled the string up the bubble gum was gone and the fish was grinning up at them. "Hey, fish," Kevin shouted. "You have my gum!"

The fish opened his big mouth and blew the biggest, puffiest purple bubble that the children had ever seen.

"Awesome!" said Kevin, as the fish swam far out into the ocean. Uncle Farley's teeth were STILL in his mouth.

"I'll get my mom," said Emma. "She's a dentist. She pulls teeth all the time." So off Emma went to the golf course to look for her mom.

Emma's mom came at once. She walked out into the water. "Fish," she called. And:

The Fabulous Fish with the freckled fin
Swam back into the harbour again
He wore Uncle Farley's teeth as if
They belonged to him.

"Open wide," she said. The fish opened his mouth wide, then with Uncle Farley's teeth bit down on the dentist's hand.

"Ouch!" said Emma's mom, and ran away.

"Rats!" said Emma, as the big fish swam far out into the ocean again. Uncle Farley's teeth were STILL in his mouth.

"My dad is a policeman," said Natasha. "He can have that fish arrested. I'll go look for him."

Natasha looked all over town, and it took her nearly two hours to find him.

Natasha's dad walked out into the water. "Fish," he called, "this is the police. Come back to shore with your teeth out." And:

The Fabulous Fish with the freckled fin
Swam back into the harbour again
He wore Uncle Farley's teeth as if
They belonged to him.

The fish blew another large purple bubble.

"Cool," said Natasha. But then the bubble broke, and gum went all over her dad. There was gum on his badge, gum all over his uniform, and even gum on his face.

"OOPS!" said Natasha.

"Eweee!" said her dad, and went to find a donut shop.

The fish swam far out into the ocean again. Uncle Farley's teeth were STILL in his mouth.

"My dad is the mayor," said Willie. "My mom says he can get people to do anything."

Willie knew *exactly* where to find his dad. He was home watching cartoons like he did every afternoon.

"Fish," he called. "Fish, come here. This is a meeting." And:

The Fabulous Fish with the freckled fin
Swam back into the harbour again
He wore Uncle Farley's teeth as if
They belonged to him.

"I promise to clean the garbage from the ocean," said the Mayor. "I promise that from now on the fish will be the most important of all the animals." And he promised, and he promised, and he promised. "Okay," he said. "How much will it cost me?"

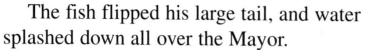

The fish flipped his large tail, and water splashed down all over the Mayor.

"Holy cow!" said Willie. "Look at Dad's suit."

"Humph," said the Mayor, and stomped off. The big fish swam far out into the ocean again. Uncle Farley's teeth were STILL in his mouth.

It was getting late. D'Arcy was all alone on the beach. Three hours had almost passed and Uncle Farley would be awake in exactly thirteen minutes.

"I have to get Uncle Farley's teeth back," D'Arcy told herself. She thought of things she could do. "I could wait until the fish is asleep. But that would take too long. I could try to make him sneeze." But she didn't know how.

D'Arcy walked out into the water. "Fish," she called. And:

The Fabulous Fish with the freckled fin
Swam back into the harbour again
He wore Uncle Farley's teeth as if
They belonged to him.

"Fish," D'Arcy said. "The teeth belong to my Uncle Farley. He will be waking up from his nap in...OH MY!...in nine more minutes."

The fish looked her square in the eye. "Now let me get this straight," he said. "These are your Uncle Farley's teeth? They've been in someone else's mouth?"

D'Arcy nodded.

"UGGGGGGGH!" said the fish. "Why didn't anyone tell me in the first place?"

The fish flipped his large tail, then swam far out into the ocean again. Uncle Farley's teeth were...

...safe in D'Arcy's pocket, and she raced home before Uncle Farley woke up.